THE
AMUSEMENT PARK
FROM THE
BLACK LAGOON®

Reading Is Snow Much Fun!

To: Kade

From: Ms Gusdal
Gr.3

Get more monster-sized laughs from

The Black Lagoon®

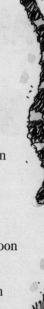

THE
AMUSEMENT PARK
FROM THE
BLACK LAGOON®

OH NO!

by Mike Thaler
Illustrated by Jared Lee

SCHOLASTIC INC.

For Mika Jean—a very special person!
M.T.

To Gary and Phyllis Nischwitz
—J.L.

ISBN 978-0-545-61641-6

Text copyright © 2014 by Mike Thaler
Illustrations copyright © 2014 by Jared D. Lee Studio, Inc.

12 11 10 9 8 7 6 5 4 3 2 1   14 15 16 17 18 19/0

Printed in the U.S.A.   40
First printing, April 2014

SUPER
GIGANTIC →
COOTIE

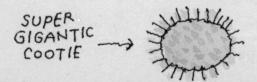

SUN →

CONTENTS

← NOT AMUSED

CHAPTER 1
I AM NOT AMUSED

"It's time for our end-of-the-semester field trip," announces Mrs. Green. "All right, class, where would you like to go?"

Everyone's hand goes up.

"Yes, Eric?" Mrs. Green calls on him.

"Dizzyland, Dizzyland, Dizzyland."

Mrs. Green writes "Dizzyland" on the blackboard.

"Derek," says Mrs. Green.

"Dizzyland, Dizzyland, Dizzyland."

← HAVING FUN

GNATS →

Z

EYEBALL

YUMMY.

BEDBUGS

7

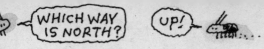

"Penny?" Mrs. Green calls on her.

"I'd like to go to Dizzyland, too." She smiles.

Mrs. Green looks at me.

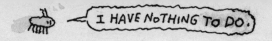

"Hubie?"

"What about the petting zoo?" I ask.

"BOO, BOO, BOO!" yells the class.

HUBIE SLIDES DOWN IN HIS SEAT

DID HE REALLY SAY THAT?

Eric raises his hand. "Hubie can pick whatever he wants, no matter how wimpy it is," he says.

Mrs. Green writes "Petting Zoo" on the blackboard. Needless to say, the vote is 22 to 1.

WHAT ABOUT A PETTING ANT HILL?

I LIKE THAT.

CHAPTER 2
BUSTED

AARDVARK →

"What's the matter with you?" Eric asks me on the bus ride home.

"The petting zoo has a new aardvark," I say.

11

TAKE ME FOR A RIDE.

"Are you out of your gourd? Dizzyland has all new rides. The Cyclone, the Hurricane, the Tornado," says Eric, jumping up and down in his seat.

"Do you realize those are all the names of natural disasters?" I answer.

IT IS SAID THAT A RUSHING TORNADO SOUNDS LIKE A FREIGHT TRAIN.

"You're scared of it," shouts Eric. "Hubie's afraid to go to Dizzyland!"

CHAPTER 3
IF THE TRUTH BE KNOWN

When I get home, I talk to Mom about it. "Eric's right, Mom. . . . I am afraid to go. I fall off swings. The slide is too high for me. I get dizzy in elevators."

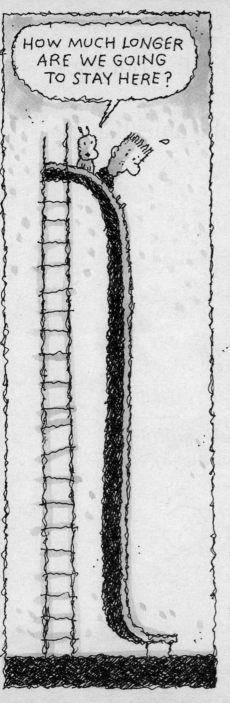

"But, Hubie, all the rides are very safe," Mom says.

"Safe up until the time that I go on them!"

"Hubie, that's silly. That hardly
ever happens, and besides, you
could fall out of your own bed."

"I do."

 FOOTNOTE: THE FERRIS WHEEL WAS INVENTED
IN 1893 BY MR. FERRIS. THE BUMPER CAR
WAS NOT INVENTED BY
MR. BUMPER.

CHAPTER 4
X MARKS THE SPOT

Why can't I be brave?

Why can't I be fearless?

I will be!

I'll watch the Super X-Sports on TV.

20

Wow! There are kids my age doing triple flips on bikes, motorcycles, and skateboards.

Going up looks easy—it's coming down that's the problem.

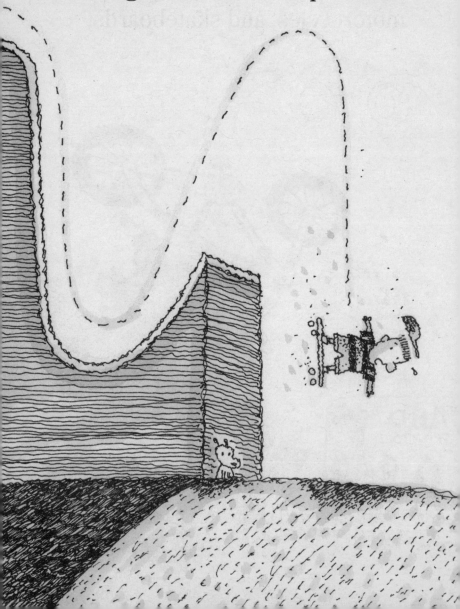

I decide I'd rather have my head in the clouds . . . but my feet on the ground.

23

CHAPTER 5
A SCREAM OF A DREAM

That night I have a *parkmare*. My class arrives at Dizzyland and goes straight to Disaster World.

HAVE YOU SEEN MY FIN?

IT'S ON THE NEXT PAGE.

I'm in the front of the line to ride the Cyclone, the Hurricane, and the Tornado! I try to let the girls go first, but everyone pushes me on the rides.

RIDE AT YOUR OWN RISK. GOOD LUCK!

WEAR YOUR SAFETY BELT, IF THERE IS ONE.

ENTER RIDES HERE

AID STATION →

BABY CLOUD

POPCORN

← POPCORN

I'm strapped in and going up, up, up. There's a skeleton sitting next to me eating popcorn!

"This is a great ride. It's my second time," says the skeleton. Then it offers me some snacks.

Suddenly, the bottom drops out and I'm falling, falling, falling with a bunch of bones . . . falling right out of bed.

My heart is pounding like a drum. I am not looking forward to tomorrow!

CHAPTER 6
POTTY LUCK

Everyone meets in the school parking lot. All the kids are excited except for me. I didn't even eat any breakfast so there wouldn't be a lot to throw up.

Eric slaps me on the back. "Big day, big fella!"

On the bus, even the girls are excited.

"I'm going on Rolling Thunder," says Penny.

"I'm going on Pancakes," says Doris.

"What's Pancakes?" I ask.

"You get flattened just like a pancake." Doris smiles.

"Oh, great," I sigh.

31

The one ride no one will go on is Galactic Disaster.

"I hear it's the scariest ride in the universe," says Eric.

"You have to sign a waiver," says Freddy.

"What's a waiver?" I ask.

"If anything happens to you, your parents can't sue the park."

"Oh, great!" I say.

I'D LIKE FOR YOU TO PAY HIS HOSPITAL BILL.

WE'RE SORRY ABOUT YOUR SON'S ACCIDENT, BUT HERE'S THE WAIVER HE SIGNED.

INVOICE

AMUSEMENT PARK MANAGER

"We're here!" shouts T-Rex, slamming on the brakes.

All the other kids jump off the bus. I slowly climb down the stairs.

"What's the matter, Hubie?" asks Mrs. Green.

"I think I'm bus-sick," I mumble.

"So where are you going?" asks Mrs. Green.

"To the bathroom," I answer.

BE CAREFUL, HUBIE.

I'LL KEEP AN EYE ON HIM.

OH, BOY.

HAND ← OVER STOMACH

I'M SO HAPPY.

35

CHAPTER 7
AVOID THE VOID

I start to wander around the amusement park looking for the bathroom. Along the way, I see a few carnival games. *These don't look so bad*, I think. I try to ring the bell with a hammer. It only reaches "wimp."

I try shooting free throws. I miss the backboard completely.

I try knocking over the milk bottles and I come up empty.

Finally, I get in the line for the bathroom. The line moves slowly. Maybe it'll take a long time. Maybe I could spend all day riding the toilet.

RIDER →

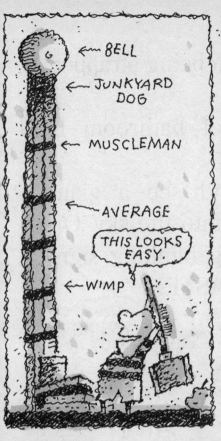

Suddenly, I am being strapped into a capsule.

"What kind of bathroom is this?" I yell.

I look up and see a giant tower going up into the sky. On top there's a big blinking sign: GALACTIC DISASTER.

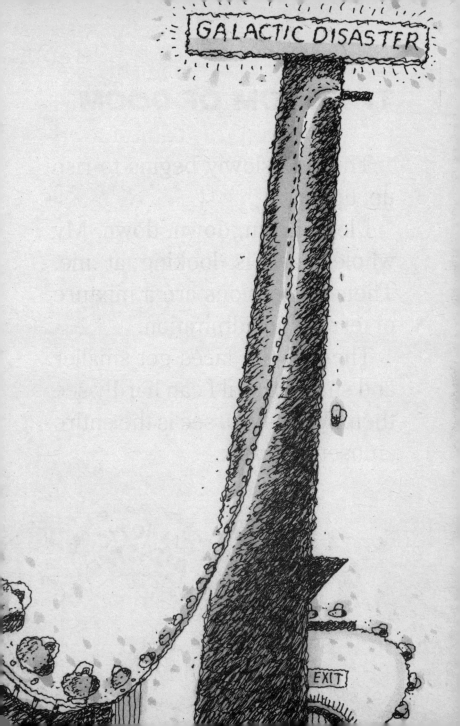

CHAPTER 8
THE BOOM OF DOOM

The ride slowly begins to rise up, up, up. . . .

I look down, down, down. My whole class is looking at me. Their expressions are a mixture of terror and admiration.

Then all the faces get smaller and smaller until I can hardly see them. What I *can* see is the entire amusement park.

I can see the yellow school bus way out in the parking lot. I can see all the rides. I can even see my house from here!

I feel like a bird. I feel like Superman. I feel a lot better.

"This ride's not so baaaad!" Just then, the bottom drops out and I rush toward Earth. It feels like I'm racing the wind to the ground.

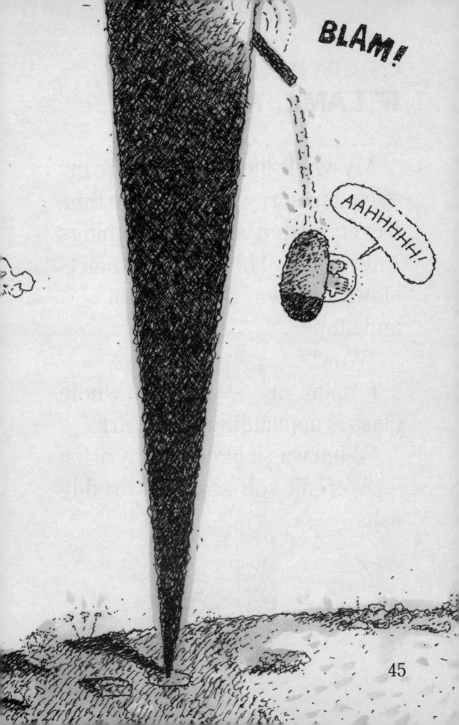

CHAPTER 9
IF LAME, NO FAME

My whole life flashes before my eyes. I'm sorry about all the time I ever wasted and all the things I never did. Then the ride starts slowing down, down, down . . . and stops.

"Wow!"

I open my eyes. The whole class is applauding. Even Eric.

"What was it like?" Penny asks.

"Weren't you scared?" Freddy asks.

FASTER
THAN A
JET
AIRPLANE ——→

"Can I have your autograph?" Mrs. Green asks.

Cool Hubie the daredevil just smiles . . . and faints.

49

CHAPTER 10
THE FUN HOUSE

In the afternoon, we all go into the fun house. Everyone wants me to lead since I am the hero of the day.

We all hold hands as we start down a dark tunnel. We hear weird noises, but it's only Eric being silly. Suddenly, skeletons with flashing red eyes jump out of the walls and bats swoop from the ceiling. I press on like Christopher Columbus or Admiral Byrd.

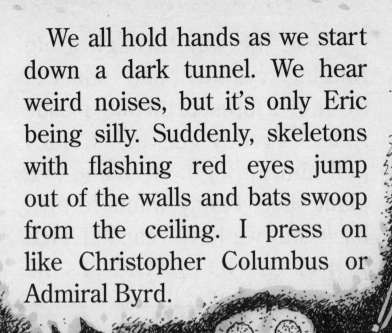

MOVE ON!

I lead the way through a big rotating cylinder and squeeze through a forest of turning plastic rollers. Freddy gets stuck, but I pull him through. We come to a giant slide. Penny wants to turn back, but we have reached THE POINT OF NO RETURN, as the sign on the wall tells us.

I yell "Geronimo!" and jump down the slide.

All the kids follow and we wind up in a big pile at the bottom. We untangle ourselves as the floor begins to move.

PLAYING
POSSUM
↙

53

CHAPTER 11
THE HALL OF TALL

"Are we having fun yet?" asks Freddy. Well, the fun doesn't start until we all land in THE HALL OF MIRRORS.

Freddy goes on an instant diet, and I look like a giant. Penny has a pinhead, and Doris has spider legs. She does a little dance for us, and we all laugh.

WHOA!

55

Finally, I find the way out and we land back in the sunshine.

"That was fun," I say. "Let's do it again!"

We go through the fun house ten times, until they finally tell us the park is closing. Each time we do it, it becomes less scary. I am sad when we have to leave.

CHAPTER 12
ZERO TO HERO

Later we go out for pizza. Everyone has stories about the rides they went on.

Doris loved Pancakes and rode it ten times.

OH, BOY!

SYRUP →

SHORT STACK

Derek did Dead Man's Drop
once and told the story ten times.

Freddy ate a mountain of cotton
candy, seven hot dogs, and three
shakes.

But I'm the real star. I have to keep telling the story. Every time I do, the tower gets higher until I can see the whole Earth.

"Wow!" everyone cheers.

What a day! What a ride! What a hero!

61

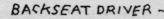

CHAPTER 13
NO FEAR

From that day on, I wasn't afraid of any rides. I go on roller coasters nonstop. I go down the slide backward. I even got a skateboard. But I always wear a helmet, goggles, elbow pads, and four knee pads.

ELBOW PADS

HELMET

GOGGLES

KNEE PADS

SKATE DOG

GOOD SKATEBOARD

I may be fearless, but I'm not foolish.